The Lori Biscuit Chronicles

Lori Biscuit Saves Grandstaffville

The Musical Detective

Kyri Demby

ROYAL MEDIA
PUBLISHING

Royal Media and Publishing
P. O. Box 4321
Jeffersonville, IN 47131
502-802-5385
royalmediapublishing@gmail.com
www.royalmediaandpublishing.com

ISBN- 978-1-955501-12-5

Randy E. Gray II, Cover illustration
Reggie Watkins, Cover design

Publishing in the U. S. A

Dedication

This book is dedicated to my Mother, Linda Brown and my Sisters Kimberly James and Bernez Henley.
All the other women in my family!

Acknowledgements

Thank you to Randy E. Gray II and Reggie Watkins.

Table of Contents

CHAPTER ONE

Lori Biscuit Captures Fortissimo

For more than twenty years, the city of Grandstaffville remained a quiet town. But recent events were about to change the peace that fourteen-year-old Lori Biscuit and the people of Grandstaffville once knew.

At exactly 5AM, a loud sound spread through the city, waking everyone up from sleep. It was a sound that no child below the age of fifteen had ever heard. Well, except Lori, of course. Dr. Maestro, her guardian, had told her the complete history of the city of Grandstaffville, including its fair share of monsters. But as the sound came, Lori was fast asleep in her room, completely unaware of the size of the damage that was about to be let loose on her beloved Grandstaffville.

Out in the city, there was confusion everywhere. People opened the windows of their houses to look into the streets below to see what was happening. There was no sign of anything wrong. Suddenly, there was a loud crash coming from Alto Avenue, an avenue not too far away from the Orchestra Zoo. The Orchestra Zoo was one of the most popular but feared places in Grandstaffville.

"Not again!" an elderly woman from up the window said and shut the window quickly. The elderly woman was Anna McQueen, a former Senator. She had seen this before, too.

Not long after Anna McQueen disappeared from the window, people ran out from the street where the BOOM sound came from.

A second sound came again, followed by the sound of a building crashing down to earth.

"Run! It's out!" a man in his early forties screamed. "Fortissimo is out. Run for your lives, people of Grandstaffville!"

As soon as those who stood by the street side heard the name "Fortissimo", they took to their heels. Fortissimo's name was the closest physical thing that defined danger and destruction to the people of Grandstaffville. Everyone knew its story, including children and others who were not born when Fortissimo began its era of destruction.

Fortissimo was one of the most dangerous and largest animals in the Orchestra Zoo. And now he had escaped. He was not an animal one could easily use for recreation. He could only be displayed under strict control. When he got mad, he could shatter everything in his way, including buildings and trees. And he could do this with only his feet! When he opened his mouth, he could melt all the cars. And when a person got too close to him, he could blow their eardrum out simply with his breath. That was why the parents in Grandstaffville always advised their children, "Stay in the house and put in your earplugs." This was an instruction that the children in Grandstaffville learned as soon as they could understand words.

For years, the people of Grandstaffville did everything possible to prevent Fortissimo from escaping the zoo. How he was now suddenly on the street, would remain a mystery to them.

***

Fortissimo, giving out the loudest groan possible for an animal of his size, changed direction and walked down Main Street, one of the busiest streets in Grandstaffville. The Grandstaffville Central Library was located on Main Street.

"Out of the way," one of the Grandstaffville policemen ordered. "Out of the way. He's stepping on everything." As soon as he said that, he turned and saw a seven-year-old boy on the street, about a hundred meters away from him. The kid's name is Denver and he was looking for his mother.

The policeman was confused about what to do when he saw Denver. He knew that before he could reach the boy, Fortissimo would have stepped on him. He was about to give up on the screaming boy when he saw a girl run quickly in Denver's direction and pick him up just before Fortissimo's large feet landed on the exact spot. The girl was Lori Biscuit.

Thirty minutes ago, Lori was not aware of what was happening in the city until a call came through to her. The call found her when she was in the middle of breakfast. Like her guardian, Lori hated to be interrupted when she was eating. Her motto when it came to food was simple. "Eat healthy and be merry. No one knows what tomorrow brings. But when she noticed it was the emergency phone ringing, she immediately picked up the phone and answered.

It was the town mayor, his voice full of desperation and plea. "Lori, I'm sorry to interrupt you this early morning. But this is an emergency. Grandstaffville needs you once again!"

"Well, what is it this time, Mr. Mayor?" Lori asked, looking around the room for any sign of Dr. Maestro. Now that he was getting old, Lori found herself getting worried over him at the slightest reasons. More often than not, she wondered how her life would have turned out if she hadn't met him, or he hadn't met her.

When Dr. Maestro brought the four-year-old Lori Biscuit home with him to Grandstaffville ten years ago, no one knew where he brought her from. All they could remember was that their celebrated scientist went for an international symposium and returned with a child wearing an oversized hat on her head. Grandstaffville was divided when it came to Lori's identity.

On one side, some of the townspeople believed Lori was Dr. Maestro's daughter, from a woman none of them had ever met and who had probably died in childbirth. They even went as far as to say that the hat Lori always wore was the only souvenir she had to remind her of her mother.

Others, on the other hand, believed that Lori was perhaps Dr. Maestro's niece. But no one had ever seen Dr. Maestro with a wife or a brother or a sister to believe the story. At last, the people of

Grandstaffville accepted the mystery that surrounded Lori and her guardian.

As the years went by, Dr. Maestro trained Lori Biscuit in the art of using sound as weaponry against monsters. He suspected that, after two decades of peace, Grandstaffville would soon be troubled by monsters again. He wanted someone to be fully prepared to stop the destruction of the town one day. By the time Lori was twelve, she had become even more stronger and skillful at using musical weapons than her guardian. Before she was fourteen, she was already a hero in the city of Grandstaffville. Every child, mother, and father knew her name. It was said that Lori had more medals from the Mayor's office more than the entire Grandstaffville Police Department.

"Well, one of the animals escaped from the Orchestra Zoo this morning and if he's not stopped, he will destroy our whole town," Lori heard the mayor explaining across the other side of the line.

"Well, which animal was it?" Lori asked.

"It is FORTISSIMO!!!" the mayor cried.

That explains the Boom! Boom!! Boom!!! sounds I've been hearing, Lori thought.

"I will get there as soon as possible," she told the mayor and hung up.

When Lori finished talking with the mayor on the phone, she ran down to the Underground to meet Dr. Maestro. The Underground was Dr. Maestro's making. It was a secret place where every kind of musical weapon was planned and invented.

"Ah! See who's here," Dr. Maestro said, opening his arms to embrace Lori. "Now, I know why you're here. You'll need this," he said, giving a bag of gadgets to Lori. The bag contained Dynamic Tasers. Lori listened quietly as Dr. Maestro took the weapons and instructed her.

"See this?" he asked, lifting one of the weapons. "This here, is the Crescendo Ray. With this, you can make any sound louder."

"And what about this?" Lori asked, touching another weapon.

"Aha!" Dr. Maestro exclaimed. "This, right here, is the Decrescendo Ray. And, I guess you already know what it does?"

"Makes sound gets softer," Lori replied.

"Yes, yes," Dr. Maestro replied, putting his hand into his bag. When his hand emerged, it was holding an object that looked like a stick.

"What's this? And why aren't you leaving it in the bag?" Lori asked, confused.

"This is the most powerful weapon against any villain. It is called the Baton."

"Then, I will need it," Lori said, reaching for the Baton.

"Not so fast," Dr. Maestro said, taking it away from Lori's grasp. "Not today, at least," he added quickly when he saw the disappointed look on his protégé's face. "One day, you will need this. When the day comes, no one will tell you. Not even me. Only you will know. Now, go. Save our city!"

Dressed in her iconic blue pants, brown cloak and hat, Lori hurried into the city with her bag of gadgets, in the direction of the Symphony Hall. The mayor was already there waiting for her.

"He's just left the town library!" the mayor informed her. "He's heading here, for the Symphony Hall."

"Then, we have to work fast," Lori advised. "We can cut him off at Bar Line Park. But first, you have to make sure that no one is in the way. I don't want to see any child, man, or woman close to me. My weapons are too powerful for a human. Keep everyone out of the way!"

In a minute, the city policemen went about working, ordering and taking everyone out of the way. It was around this time that Lori saw Denver on the street and rushed to save him before Fortissimo pounced on him.

Fortissimo was a monster the size of which Lori had never confronted before. Twenty feet tall, he opened his mouth in all his glory and melted the trees and the cars before him. Lori threw herself on the opposite side of the road, away from Fortissimo's breath. Fortissimo faced her direction again and breathed out. Lori plunged herself away from his breath again, dropping her bag of gadgets on the ground, about fifty meters away. Not giving up, Fortissimo jumped as high as he could into the air.

Lori knew she had to stop Fortissimo before he landed on the ground. Lifting into the air was Fortissimo's greatest weapon. Whenever he went off the ground and landed again, there would be an earthquake, the likes of which Grandstaffville had never seen before.

Quickly, just as the monster was descending, Lori ran across the street divide toward her bag of gadgets. She glided through the ground, took the bag and retrieved the Decrescendo Ray. As Fortissimo was breaking into the ground from one side of the tower of the Symphony Hall, Lori directed the mouth of the Decrescendo Ray in the direction of his face and pulled the trigger.

The sound completely zapped the raging Fortissimo in the air. His ears, mouth, and nose all opened wide in his fury, then completely began to shrink until he landed softly on the ground. He made a soft sound that appeared as if a large animal was peacefully sleeping.

Lori watched the shrunken Fortissimo as he completely transformed into a very soft pianissimo. She turned her head and looked at the damage around her. She wondered how such a tiny thing could be capable of this enormous destruction.

"Look!" a little girl holding unto her mother's dress shouted. "The big thing is no more! Look!"

Lori went over and picked the soft pianissimo up and gave it to the mayor.

"Keep it very safe in the Orchestra Zoo this time around," she instructed.

"I sure will see to that," he said as he smiled and patted Lori on the back. "Thank you, child. Glad to know we can always count on you," he added and began to walk away.

"Mayor," Lori called.

The mayor turned. "Yes?"

"I mean, very safe," Lori repeated, looking concerned.

"I know," he said and left.

Gradually, Main Street became filled with the people of Grandstaffville, shouting for joy, "Lori Biscuit has saved the day again!"

Someone touched Lori. She turned and looked into the eyes of Denver, smiling. She picked up the little boy and walked into the crowd of people, saying, "I believe that most of you have not yet have your breakfast. But now it's time for celebration. As I always say, eat healthy and be merry. No one knows what tomorrow brings'"

The people of Grandstaffville laughed. How they adored their hero!

About a hundred meters from where she stood, Dr. Maestro looked at his protégé with pride and sadness in his eyes. As the city was wrapped in celebration, he suspected that someone was behind the sudden escape of Fortissimo from the Zoo, and that he would not be the last monster the city of Grandstaffville would be seeing.

If only he were wrong.

CHAPTER TWO

Saving Mark

After the defeat of Fortissimo, only a few numbers of parents in Grandstaffville took it as the sign of evil things to come. The rest thought that since Lori had successfully defeated the villain, there was nothing more to be afraid of. Life in Grandstaffville continued as normal. Children, in their large numbers, continued to frequent the Bar Line Park to play. The Bar Line Park was one of the most popular public places in Grandstaffville. Its citizens usually came there to socialize with one another and to catch up with the latest gossip in town.

But on this particular Saturday, barely forty-eight hours after the defeat of Fortissimo, something terrible that resembled nothing of its kind in a long time was about to change.

A sharp soundwave drifted from the high branches of the oaks that littered the horizon of Bar Line Park, almost like the screech of fingernails scratching a chalk board. The soundwave could be seen. It looked like invisible waves of water flowing on the beach. Some of the older people stopped speaking and listened carefully. When they heard everything was hushed and still, they resumed their chatter, forgetting about the sharp sound.

The soundwave, becoming even braver, suddenly moved toward the crowd of children playing some great distance away from their parents.

A little boy of six raised his head, laughing as he looked at the blue of the sky. When he saw a large body wrapped in the moderate light of the oak leaves coming downward, his eyes quickly fled towards his thirteen-year-old brother who was chasing after another boy. The smile on his face washed out gradually.

"Mark, something is coming behind you," he cried and began to run to his parents.

"Shut up, Kelvin," Mark said and continued with his chase.

By then, Kelvin had already drawn the attention of his father, a slightly overweight man who seemed to be the life of the small group sitting around a table. Despite his body, Andy was one of the bravest men in the Grandstaffville Police Department and quite respected all over the city. No one knew what had happened between them in the past, but Andy and the Mayor of Grandstaffville could just never see eye-to-eye.

When he heard Kelvin shouting and pointing in his elder brother's direction, he sensed there must be danger. For Kelvin, on more than one occasion, had appeared to be one of those gifted children who could tell when something bad was about to happen. Quickly, he sprinted towards his first son, shouting his name, "Mark!"

It was too late.

The sharp soundwave bolted out of the air and yanked Andy from off the ground before finally releasing him. Andy landed with a thud, groaned heavily and then fainted. Everything happened within seconds.

The sharp soundwave, still in its sudden movement, changed its direction towards Mark again. A crowd of screaming and terrified children, men, and women also ran in every direction imaginable, away from the horror their eyes had just seen.

Even at Mark's age, no one needed to tell him he was in trouble now. He commanded his legs and began to speed out of his sight. No child in Grandstaffville could run faster than Mark. But he did not go a step farther when the sharp soundwave closed in behind him. The sound was deafening. Mark brought his two palms to protect his ears from its attack, but it was worthless.

Some of the parents who were running stopped in their tracks and turned to the screaming Mark. Before their very eyes, they later narrated to anyone who cared to listen, Mark's body began to move quickly in a circle, about thirty feet off the ground, and then suddenly disappeared. In their entire lifetime, no one had ever seen anything like what had just happened. Except in a movie, of course!

The mayor was the first to receive the news. Lori, as always, was in the Underground with Dr. Maestro when his call came in.

"Dr. Maestro here," he answered.

"Doctor, there's a problem at Bar Line Park. Is Lori there?"

"Yes, she is," Dr. Maestro affirmed, looking at Lori whose attention was far away from him. "Okay, I will tell her right away."

Dr. Maestro sighed deeply as he walked back into the workshop table. "I have bad news, Lori," he said, trying to read the expression on her face.

"Something bad happened at Bar Line?" Lori asked?

"So you heard?"

"No, just that. That's all."

"A boy was picked up by Axidental about ten minutes ago," Dr. Maestro said, turning his face away.

Lori knew the look on his face. It was the look he always had whenever he was about to hide something from her.

"And?" she asked, peering into her guardian's face curious.

"I am sorry, Lori," Dr. Maestro began, "the missing boy is Mark."

"Mark Andrew?" Lori said, not believing her ears.

"Yes."

The workshop suddenly appeared to be closing in on Lori. She quickly ran out of there, breathing heavily. Dr. Maestro decided not to go after her.

Five years ago, when Lori first came to Grandstaffville, the first true friend she made was Mark. And he still was. As a child, there was something about Lori that made other children her age uncomfortable. It was not her hat, which was always on her head. It was certainly not the blue pants which she seemed to have many pairs. It was also not her long, strapless cloak of deep brown. It was not the fact that she hardly said a word to anyone. It was not because she lived with the even weirder Dr. "Stranger." It was simply because there was "something" more to her, something that no one in Grandstaffville could pin down to their level of understanding.

And so they teased her. From school, to the streets of Grandstaffville, right into the Echo Avenue where Dr. Maestro lived.

But only one boy saw that Lori acted as if she did not care how many times she was mocked, she was in need of friendship, like any child her age. That boy was Mark. As a chubby boy who wore glasses, Mark knew what it meant to be jeered at and bullied and shamefaced. The kids around Grandstaffville called him "The Big Blind Boy" even though he was not blind.

One day, after school hours, Mark waited for Lori outside the school gate. He stood there, still, casting a long glance through his glasses at her as she passed by. Lori, noticing, narrowed her eyes at him, shrugged and continued walking. Mark followed her, still silent.

Lori was tempted to turn and lash out at him. But he still had not said anything to her. He was merely following her.

When she cut the road into Echo Avenue and saw Mark still on her trail, she decided she had had enough. "What do you want?"

The words came out from her mouth so angrily that Mark stopped, his eyes squinting to see her clearly.

"I-I... I'm sorry," Mark stammered. "I only want to be your friend."

Lori chuckled, finding the whole thing amazing. She cocked her head to the other side and mumbled, "Well, did you have to walk a long distance for that?" She smiled then walked over and led Mark by the hand. Together, they covered the rest of the distance to Lori's house.

"You think the other boys would laugh at us for being friends?" Mark asked.

Lori looked at him sideways. "They will get used to it," she said, grinning.

It continued like that between them. Each day after school, Lori and Mark would walk home side by side. They did almost everything together. They talked about everything. When she had finally come to trust him completely, Mark was the first and only person that Lori told about her training at mastering musical weapons.

Even Dr. Maestro, who never entertained strangers in his place, gradually warmed up to Mark. He would open the door and smile warmly at Mark whenever he came every Saturday to take Lori to the Bar Line Park.

Andy and Maggie, on the other hand, had no problem with their son always being seen in the company of the Maestro Girl, as the people of Grandstaffville called Lori.

"Why are you always wearing this?" Mark asked one day when they were returning from school.

"What do you mean?"

"Your hat," Mark repeated, wishing he had not asked in the first place.

"I don't know," Lori answered, refusing to look at Mark's eyes. "I have no reason to wear it."

"Well, it looks plenty good on you," Mark said, and quickly added, "You know, the fascinating thing about you is that you are different. Which is a good thing."

"That's the nicest thing anyone ever said to me," Lori said genuinely.

"I should be saying that often then," Mark said, laughing.

Lori plowed her fingers into the tender muscles of his hands as they ran down Echo avenue.

That was five years ago. And Mark had never stopped being her friend. Even when she became the hero of Grandstaffville, they still maintained their friendship.

Dr. Maestro was still in the workshop when Lori suddenly emerged, her eyes red. It was obvious she had been crying.

Lori said nothing to him as she picked her bag of gadgets and began to go out.

"You will need these," his voice stopped her just before she reached the door. Lori turned and looked at him, holding a set of modified, pre-molded earplugs.

"The animal that took your friend is Axidentol. Like Fortissimo, he has been in the Orchestra Zoo for years. I have a feeling that someone is freeing these dangerous animals for a selfish purpose." Dr. Maestro sounded sorrowful as his face looked through the wall, as if to find the culprit. "But enough of that now," he continued. "First, you must understand that Axidentol takes people by paralyzing them with his sharp sound, which is always rapid and efficient so you can never tell where it is coming from. If you're not protected, he can dominate your entire body through the combination of his sound. The destruction is total. The only way to stop him is to draw closer to him and then shoot him with the Pitch Modulator."

"Which is why I need the earplugs," Lori reasoned.

"Yes. Now, let's try this," Dr. Maestro said, handing over the earplugs to Lori.

Lori collected the earplugs then pulled her earlobe away from her head and inserted the plugs.

When she did that, Dr. Maestro took a hammer from his desk and hit the closest metal he could find.

Lori stared at him, unmoved. He signaled her to remove the plugs.

"Did you hear anything?" he asked as soon as her ears were freed.

"No."

"Excellent! Very excellent!"

There was the sound of the workshop door opening. Dr. Maestro and Lori raised their head toward the direction of the sound, alert at the approaching footsteps. Andy and Maggie's faces slowly appeared in full view as they descended the stairs of the workshop.

"Ah!" Dr. Maestro sighed with relief.

"Sorry, Dr. Maestro," Andy apologized. "We thought we might find you two here."

Dr. Maestro and Lori could see the pain on the faces of Andy and Maggie. Maggie dashed quickly to Lori's side and took her hands.

"Please, return my Mark to me safe. Please," Maggie pleaded and broke down in tears. Andy walked over to his wife and disengaged her from Lori's body into his warm embrace. That was when the emergency phone rang again.

Dr. Maestro took the call and listened sadly as the mayor delivered his message.

The rest of the three people in the room looked at him, curious.

"Twelve more children have disappeared," he declared, sitting heavily on the nearest chair to him.

Lori went over to him and raised his head.

"I will get all of them back, I promise."

Dr. Maestro looked into her eyes and felt as if the shadows that were never there in all the years he had raised her were pooling in on them. How could his Lori, his sweet little Lori, be able to protect a city like Grandstaffville alone? "Lori?" he called when she opened the exit door.

Lori stopped.

"Come back alive," he said in a whisper.

Lori smiled. "I will," she assured him and gently pushed the door open.

She had her best friend and a dozen of kids to save.

CHAPTER THREE

The Price of Friendship

All Mark could remember was that he was playing when he felt himself being swallowed by a heavy object. He could remember hearing his father screaming his name. He could remember there was a sound that seemed to have a form, lifting him into the air. And then he was gone. Just like that!

The next time he woke up, he was in a very dark room. He heard the screams of other children echoing off from afar. There was someone panting a few feet away from him. He stretched his eyes as far as he could to see who it was. It was obvious he was not alone in the room. He felt around in the darkness for his glasses. That was when he felt a hand touch him. He turned quickly, frightened by the touch. It was Lola, a six-year-old girl. Her face looked drowsy, like someone who was about to faint.

Lola's father, Desmond, was his father's colleague at the Grandstaffville Police Department.

Unknown to Mark, Lola's body was slumped against the wall, a trail of blood dripping down from her left hand. While rushing to pick up the rest of the children, Axidentol had violently dropped her and disappeared again. As she rolled on the floor, her hand hit a sharp metal object, tearing a part of her flesh off. When she realized she was also losing a lot of blood from a cut on her upper left arm, she called out to Mark.

Mark's finger sank to the floor, searching for his glasses. He found them five feet away from him and put them on. "Are you all right, Lola?" Mark asked when he saw her bleeding.

"I'm scared, Mark," Lola said, lowering her face into his big shoulders. He tore a piece of his T-shirt and dabbed it against her wounds.

"I'm fine now," she said and gently lifted her body away from the wall. She brushed her left hand softly against her wound. "Where are we?" she asked.

Mark hadn't thought of that. He stood up and looked around the room. There was only one small window that went up almost to the roof of the building. He went over to the iron door and looked outside.

"I've heard the voices of other kids," he said. "I think we are in the old, abandoned Grandstaffville Prison," he declared. "My father once told me that the last time this place was used was about forty years ago. Although I have never seen it, he said it is located on the east end of town, on the way out of Grandstaffville."

Mark wondered what the information he just told Lola would do for her. *Axidentol must be clever*, Mark thought as he realized what had happened. *Nobody would think of coming to look for us here.* The thought made him worried.

"Let me see outside, too," Lola said. It was only when she stood that they both noticed a large cut, where fresh blood was coming out. They looked at the ground. Lola's blood formed a red line from the place where she first sat to where she dragged herself to Mark's place.

"That's my blood, Mark!" she screamed, her trembling palms covering her eyes. Mark quickly stepped away from the iron door and went over to her. He gently removed her dress to see where the blood was coming from and saw that it was from a wound on her back.

He removed his already torn shirt and covered Lola's body, soaking up the blood. His eyes were teary and his voice unstable as he spoke. "It's okay, Lola," he said, wishing it was really okay. "I am here."

Lola said nothing. Then she began to cry loudly.

"Shut up!" Axidentol's voice, sounding like glass shattering, pierced through the iron door and attacked their ears. Lola and Mark covered their ears and moved back into dim light of the room.

Mark passed his fingers through Lola's long, knotted black hair. He continued to brush the strands softly to take her mind off the pain she was suffering. When he felt her temperature, her body was cold, as if she was becoming lifeless.

"Lola?" he called.

Silence.

"Lola?" he called, shaking her.

Silence again. And then a small whimper, like someone coming back to life. "Yes," Lola answered in a tired voice.

Mark dropped to the ground and lifted her face by the chin. "Stay with me, Lola," he said, his voice pleading. "Stay with me. You will, won't you?"

"I will."

"Good!" Mark said, breathing with relief.

"Mark?" Lola called.

"Yes."

"Do you think they will come and get us?" Lola asked.

"Who?"

"Our parents. Do you think my daddy and your daddy will come and get us?"

"Of course, they will," Mark assured her, embracing her in his warm arms. "Someone is coming."

He looked around the room again, his eyes motionless. The room seemed to be growing darker and creepier. The voice of a boy in another room gave out a loud cry again. Just like the last time, Axidentol's piercing voice warned him to shut up.

Mark felt Lola's head moving. He patted it and looked at the iron door, where the lights of Grandstaffville Prison passed into the room dimly.

"My friend is coming," he said and bent his head, praying silently that Lori arrived quickly, before all of them perished.

***

Meanwhile, Lori, Andy, Desmond, and a couple of other Grandstaffville policemen had been looking for the whereabouts of the missing children. They had been looking for more than hour, unsuccessfully.

"I don't think they are here in Grandstaffville," Andy said.

"And why would you say that?" Desmond asked, almost annoyed. He did not want to imagine his little Lola outside Grandstaffville all by herself and in danger.

"Well, we have searched everywhere, haven't we?" Andy asked back, angry at Desmond's tone.

"We have searched everywhere in Grandstaffville, but not outside Grandstaffville," Lori said. Her face had grown lines of concern. For the first time, she had never thought that she could be this worried about losing anyone. But Mark was not just any anyone. He was her best friend, the only friend she had in Grandstaffville, in fact. And she would do anything to make sure she brought him home. To his parents. To her. "Mark and the others, of course," she said.

"What did you say?" Andy and Desmond chorused.

Lori did not realize she had given voice to her thoughts. "I mean, we need to bring the children back," she lied.

"Well, isn't that what we're all trying to do?" Desmond asked.

"Yes," Lori replied. After some silence passed between them, she continued speaking, to Desmond. "Imagine you stole something or kidnapped someone..."

"I can't steal a thing or kidnap anyone," Desmond interrupted.

"She said 'imagine'. How hard can that be?" Andy fired. He had been looking for a way to get back at Desmond for trying to make him look stupid.

"Guys! Guys!!" Lori shouted, stomping her feet to the ground. "Focus!" She silently wished she was doing this all on her own. She loved working alone. But the mayor had insisted that he wanted them to come with her.

"Sorry," both men apologized.

"I will do the imagination," Andy added.

Lori sighed. "Now, imagine you kidnapped someone, or you stole something that everyone in Grandstaffville would be looking for you. Where would you keep them?"

"Far outside Grandstaffville," Andy said excitedly, his eyes beaming with pride like a child who had found the answer to a riddle.

"Yes," Lori answered slowly. "Let's say you don't have much time to go 'far outside Grandstaffville'," she added, mimicking Andy.

"I would keep it almost outside Grandstaffville," Desmond said.

"Where 'almost outside Grandstaffville'," Lori asked, mimicking Desmond this time.

"Any abandoned place, somewhere where no one would think of going," Andy said and then added quickly, as if something clicked in him, "At the Grandstaffville Prison! No one is been there for decades."

"That's where Axidentol is hiding them!" Lori said and ran back to the police car.

***

Ten minutes later, at the Grandstaffville Prison, Axidentol was walking around, his voice cutting through the iron bars of each room where his prisoners were. "You will be here until my master finds a purpose for you all," he said. He was still talking when he caught the lean figure of someone quickly passing through the main gate of the prison. In a second, he was at the gate.

"Who is there?" he screamed. The children in the prison rooms screamed at the effect of his voice. When no one made a single sound, he returned to his initial position.

That was when Lori appeared fully at the gate, the Pitch Modulator in her hands. Dr. Maestro told her that in his rage, Axidentol's sounds could penetrate his victim's entire body, tearing it apart. Lori had already devised a plan to keep the children safe from their captor.

The moment she knew Axidentol had seen her, she ran as far as she could through the gates. Axidentol, unseen, went after her. As soon as Andy and Desmond saw Lori running through the gates, that was all the sign they needed. They entered the prison to rescue their children. Each father screamed his child's name first.

"Lola? Lola?" Desmond shouted, going from one prison room to the other. He found some empty and then rescued any child he saw in a room.

"Mark! Mark!!" Andy shouted.

At his father's voice, Mark's head shot up, unsure if the voice he just heard was real or imagined.

"Mark!"

Mark heard the voice again. Quickly, he put Lola gently on the floor and ran back to the iron door, shaking it. "Dad? I'm here. I am here," he shouted back, banging the door with his fist.

Andy rushed to his son, opened the door and hugged him tightly. "I thought I'd lost you!"

"Not yet, Dad," Mark said, smiling. "Lola is here, too, Dad."

Andy got into the room and carried Lola's bloodied body. The three walked out of the room to find Desmond still looking into each room.

At last, he raised his head and saw Andy and his son coming toward him. And then, as if for the first time, he saw Andy carrying a child dressed in blue.

"That can't be my Lola," he cried as he covered the distance, his hands stretched forward. Andy handed over Lola to her father.

Desmond received his daughter and began to weep. "My angel. My sweet, little angel," he said between tears.

Lola's eyes gradually opened, trying to understand her environment. "Daddy," she called faintly. "Is that you?"

Desmond sighed, relieved. "Yes, sweet. It's me, your dad."

He, Andy, and Mark gathered the rest of the children and found a room to hide in while they waited for Lori.

Outside Grandstaffville Prison, Axidentol's voice went after Lori with vengeance. Everywhere he turned, the energy in his sound cracked the ground open, making Lori fall every once in a while.

When she was sure she had lured him about a three hundred meters away from the prison building, far from the children, she brought out the Pitch Modulator to set the target. But she was unable to figure out where to get the right target because she couldn't hear his sound. At last, she removed one of the earplugs. As soon as she did that, Axidentol's voice pierced through her body, lifted her off the ground, split her cloak into two, and tore her blue pants at knee level.

When Lori's face began to vibrate, she knew Axidentol was coming directly toward her. She quickly targeted him with the

Pitch Modulator and then pulled the trigger. She saw as the soundwaves streamed through the air and disappeared.

She removed her other earplug to make sure everything was normal. There was silence everywhere. Drained of energy, she picked up her hat from the ground and walked back to the prison.

Andy and Desmond led the children out of the prison when they heard the gate stop sounding. Mark was the first to rush out through the gate, heading for Lori.

When they saw each other, they hugged tightly.

"I should have come earlier," Lori apologized.

"It doesn't matter. You're here now," Mark said, holding her hands.

The group went back to Grandstaffville together and arrived at the mayor' s office, where the whole city was waiting for the return of the children.

Dr. Maestro ran to Lori as soon as she opened the car door. The people of the city turned and saw the physical state of their hero. Lori's neck was bleeding and her hair was messy. She was so weak that she had to rest on her guardian's arms for support as they walked to his car.

Everyone, especially the families affected, clasped their hands together in form of gratitude. For the first time in years, no one celebrated this victory.

As Lori and Dr. Maestro passed by the Symphony Hall, none of them heard the strange sound of a guitar coming to life. The name of the guitar was Larghissimo.

Larghissimo been used by only one person in the history of Grandstaffville, the legendary Zachary Trist. When Trist died, no one had seen his body or his guitar. Its soundtrack was so capable of inciting the greatest sadness in anyone who heard its sound. It was called *The Guitar of Sorrow*.

For the first time in fifty years, Larghissimo was about to sound again.

CHAPTER FOUR

Lori and 'The Guitar of Sorrow'

For two days after her encounter with Axidentol, Lori was in bed, sleeping.

Dr. Maestro, who had never been so scared at losing her, had ordered her to stay indoors. "You need to rest," he said. "Sometimes, I think we put too much pressure on your young shoulders."

"But I'm not complaining," Lori said, going over to embrace him. "I told you, I'll always be fine as long as I have you."

"I just want you to take care of yourself first," Dr. Maestro said.

"And I will," Lori assured her guardian.

Today, she was trying to sleep again when Mark walked into her room.

Lori was extremely happy to see him.

"I have something for you," he said without wasting time.

"What is it?" Lori asked.

"This," Mark said, handing over a drawing paper to Lori. Lori quickly unrolled the paper and stared at it; her mouth opened in surprise.

"When did you draw this?" she asked?

"The day you captured Fortissimo," Mark said, beaming with pride.

He had never thought Lori would love it. He had doubts each time he thought of giving it to her. But when Andy heard that he was going to see Lori, he called his son back. "Why don't you give Lori that thing you have been drawing for centuries, son?"

And Mark decided to do just that.

"It's lovely!" Lori said. She stared at the drawing of herself shooting the Decrescendo Ray against the raging Fortissimo while he was trying to land from the tower of the Symphony Hall. "How were you able to get this so perfectly?" she asked, still amazed.

"I don't know. I just did," Mark replied.

"Thank you, Mark," Lori said and hugged him again.

At the door, Dr. Maestro watched Lori and Mark and smiled. He turned to go back to the workshop when Lori's phone rang. He quickly walked back into the room to prevent her from picking up the phone. It was too late.

"Hello," Lori answered.

"The mayor," she whispered to Dr. Maestro who was looking at her with a bit of anger.

"You shouldn't have taken that call, child," Dr. Maestro said, walking away. "And why on God's earth does the mayor have to be the one to always call? Are the cops clueless?" he added and left the room, back to the workshop.

Lori listened quietly until the mayor finished speaking. She asked Mark to excuse her while she dressed. Quickly, she put her clothes on and went into the workshop where Mark and Dr. Maestro were waiting for her.

"The mayor just said that eight people were found outside the Symphony Hall, completely lame. He said their lips are moving as if they are singing a song that only they could hear."

Dr. Maestro sank into a chair. "So, the stories were true!" he said, almost in a whisper.

"What stories?" Lori and Mark asked at the same time.

"About the Guitar of Sorrow," Dr Maestro said.

"Zachary Trist's guitar?" Mark asked.

"Who told you that?" the old man asked, surprised.

Lori looked at Mark. It was already obvious in Grandstaffville that Mark was one of the most well-informed children in town.

"Well, I read about it in *The Book of Mysteries, Myths and Legends*, at the Grandstaffville City Library," Mark replied. "There was only a paragraph on it. That's all I know."

"Because no one wants to talk about it," Dr. Maestro said. "But what choice do we have now?" he asked, removing his jacket. "Sit."

Lori and Mark sat down as Dr. Maestro began the story of how 'The Guitar of Sorrow' got its name.

***

Even before he turned eight, everyone who knew him in the city of Grandstaffville agreed that Zachary Trist was a musical genius. Every day, he would walk around the city, going from one public gathering to the other, singing in his beautiful voice.

On his ninth birthday, Zachary's father, whom he had not seen in five years, suddenly arrived in Grandstaffville and gave his son a birthday gift. It was a very beautiful guitar, the likes of which no one in Grandstaffville had ever seen. As Trist embraced the guitar as if it was his long-lost twin, he named it Larghissimo. His attachment to Larghissimo was so strong and strange that it did not take long for the rumors to start. Some said that Trist could talk to Larghissimo and she could respond. Whether this was true or not, no one could say. But there was one thing that was true—whenever Zachary Trist sang, his songs were unusually dark and sorrowful for someone his age.

As the years passed, before their very eyes, the people watched as the young Trist became a global musical sensation, winning almost every award created for music.

Then, little by little, Trist himself began to change. One day, he called his lawyers to draft his final will. The city of Grandstaffville was shocked. No one knew of their favorite star being ill. And even though his songs were dark and sorrowful, his public life was a cheerful one, such that the people nicknamed him 'The Laughing Trist.' To complete the mockery, they nicknamed his guitar 'The Guitar of Sorrow.'

In his new and sudden will, Trist gave one part of his money to a charity that tended to war-torn children from Africa and the rest to the Grandstaffville Council for the establishment of the Symphony Hall, the Grandstaffville Melody Museum, the Grandstaffville City Library, and the Orchestra Zoo, which the *Grandstaffville Daily Reports* called 'The Trist Projects'.

As the building constructions went on, Trist gradually stopped recording music, stopped attending shows and finally stopped appearing in public altogether.

If the people of Grandstaffville were shocked, an even greater surprise was on its way. Six months after he stayed away from public life, Trist had a high wall built over his family estate, located on Echo Avenue. Each evening, the most sorrowful music could be heard coming from over the wall. No one was allowed to go in. No one wanted to go in, either.

A year later, as Grandstaffville was getting ready to commission 'The Trist Projects', Zachary Trist disappeared from the face of the Earth, never to be seen again. He was just twenty-six years old!

The night before his disappearance, according to witnesses, he was seen walking on foot towards the outskirt of Grandstaffville. Some said he sat at the edge of the city and played his guitar one last time until sunset. Others said that in Marconia, the neighboring town, some of the people heard Larghissimo's sound the night of her master's supposed death. Those who heard it were so stricken by a heavy sorrow that they could not walk again and had to be carried to their respective homes. No one knew what later became of them.

In Grandstaffville, the stories from Marconia were dismissed as the usual tales that normally followed men like Zachary Trist who had lived strange lives. Life in Grandstaffville continued, even as Zachary Trist and his beloved guitar passed into legend.

"I strongly believe that the sound those eight people heard at the Symphony Hall was Larghissimo, still mourning her master fifty years after," Dr. Maestro concluded.

"But where has she been all these years?" Lori asked.

"Same question we should ask about all the other animals and villains coming back to life after years of peace," Dr. Maestro said, his face looking tired.

"Dr. Maestro, do you think someone is behind this?" Mark asked.

"I don't 'think'. I know so."

"Is there anything we can do for the victims?" Lori asked, concerned.

"I am afraid there's nothing, child," Dr. Maestro said. "Larghissimo plays on the slowest tempo ever to get her victims. Only the Accelerando Whip could normalize her. But you have to go now before more people are affected."

"Yes," Lori answered and packed her bag of gadgets, leaving the underground workshop.

"I'm going with you," Mark said, turning to follow.

"No," Dr. Maestro's voice stopped him. "Stay here."

The two were in the workshop for more than ten minutes until Dr. Maestro went to a table to carry his jacket and put it back. That was when he noticed Lori's earplugs on the table. He looked at Mark who was pacing the workshop floor, restless.

"On second thought, you should go after her as fast as you can and give her these before it is too late. She will need them."

An extremely fast runner, Mark collected the earplugs and ran out of the workshop.

As he ran through Grandstaffville searching for Lori, he discovered that it was noticeably quiet. Even the woods in the city seemed to notice the presence of Larghissimo. No leaves were moving. The city was hushed and unnaturally calm, as if it were holding its breath for someone dead.

"Where are you, Lori?" he asked under his breath as he reached the Symphony Hall and did not find his friend there. He stood in the middle of the street, thinking hard. At last, he decided to go to Echo Avenue, to the Trist's family home.

When he reached the estate five minutes later, he saw Lori from afar, crawling on the ground, moving far away from the gate. It was as if all her strength was gone. At once, Mark ran to her and attempted to give her the earplugs. When he saw that she was growing weaker, he attached the earplugs to his ears and brought Lori's bag of gadgets to her. Lori pointed out the Accelerando Whip to him. Quickly, Mark took the whip and went into the Trist's estate.

The Trist's estate had been abandoned for decades. Everywhere Mark turned, there was overgrown grass. He found Larghissimo on the terrace, her sound as sorrowful as the reports said it would be.

In anger, he ran towards her and whipped her so hard that she gave a fast and loud shout that vibrated throughout the silence of the estate and then finally became quiet. Mark, still angry, dropped the whip and picked her up.

"You should have died with your master fifty years ago," he screamed at the unresponsive Larghissimo, hitting her on the hard terrace until she broke into two.

Tired at last, Mark raised his head and saw Lori at the gate smiling broadly at him. He took the whip and went over to her.

"Let's go home," he said, taking her hand as they left Zachary Trist's estate. "How are you feeling?" he asked.

"I feel a lot better," Lori replied. "And you?"

"I feel like a hero. Just a little tired."

"You are a hero."

"Says who?"

Lori smiled even more. "From one hero to another."

CHAPTER FIVE

The Revenge of Jack the Whisperer

"Walter, look, I've caught the ball! Yay!" Marvin screamed with delight and ran towards Walter who lifted him up.

"That's right. You're a good catcher, boy," the sixty-year-old Walter said. For more than twenty-five years, Walter had served as a housekeeper at the estate of Anna McQueen, the first woman to ever occupy a senatorial office in Grandstaffville. He had also watched the growth of all her children and grandchildren.

This weekend, as the entire McQueen family gathered to discuss important family business, Walter was relieved of his duties for the day. Well, not entirely. He had to make sure that the ever-naughty Marvin, who was always bubbly, did not disturb the meeting. Walter had been at his task for two hours.

"I think you are one amazing boy," he said to Marvin, stroking his soft, long black hair.

Marvin beamed with smiles. "Thanks, Walter," he said, letting the old man lift him high into the air. "My dad said you used to play baseball with him when he was young," Marvin said as his feet touched down.

"Oh, yeah. I actually used to play with your grandfather even. God rest his sweet soul. Did your father tell you that your grandfather was the first successful baseball player from Grandstaffville?"

"Really?" Marvin beamed.

"You didn't know?" Walter asked, enjoying the expression on Marvin's face. "Well, he was. Through his years of playing, he led his team, *The Home Guards,* to dominate the national league for more than ten years. In fact, the mayor at the time presented him with the key to the city of Grandstaffville."

"Awesome!" Marvin exclaimed.

"That's not all," Walter continued. "The president even came down to Grandstaffville to have dinner with him."

"Dinner with Grandpa?"

"*Your* grandpa," Walter emphasized. He was about to continue when he raised his head and saw Anna McQueen approaching.

"Thank you, Walter. We are done inside," Anna said. "I hope he didn't give you much trouble."

"No, madam," Walter said. "I enjoy the young master's company."

"Well, it's getting dark," Anna said and then led her seven-year-old grandson back into the house.

"Will you tell me more stories before bedtime, Walter?" Marvin turned and asked, as they climbed the stairs into the great house.

"If you want me to," Walter said.

"Promise me you will come?"

Walter put his right fist to his chest. "I promise," he said and watched as the smiling Marvin went into the house.

Two hours later when he walked into Marvin's room just before bedtime, Marvin was nowhere to be found. The clothes he'd had on were carefully placed on the bed.

At the time that Marvin was officially declared missing by the Grandstaffville Police Department, another terrible incident happened at the estate of Alex Gray, a retired NATO researcher. His heir, Christopher Gray, was on a research mission with his wife in China and had left their eight-year-old daughter, Alice, to spend the week with her grandfather. At exactly 8:15PM, Alex Gray went to her room to check if she was sleeping as she said she would. He did not find her. He called his driver and cook, and they searched the entire estate, room to room. There was still no trace of Alice. He phoned the Grandstaffville Police Department.

Both Alex Gray and Anna McQueen lived on Alto Avenue, where the richest families of Grandstaffville lived.

The cops had been at the Anna McQueen's estate without any success. Their eyes were on Walter. According to them, he was the last person to see Marvin and was also the one who broke the sad news of the boy's disappearance to the family.

Marvin's father, Orlando McQueen, gave a specific order to the cops to question the old man until he provided the whereabouts of his son.

When Anna saw the way the cops were handling Walter, she wanted none of it. "Wooden?" she called the serious-looking detective by name. It was classic Anna McQueen. She knew just about everyone in Grandstaffville by name. "What do you think you are doing?"

"Doing my job, Mrs. McQueen," Wooden replied.

"Let Walter go at once!" Anna McQueen ordered and walked to where Orlando stood discussing the case with an officer.

"Have you forgotten Walter has been in this family for twenty-five good years?" she shouted at her son, to everyone's hearing. "He may be a housekeeper, but he has honor. And I will not have that honor insulted by my son or anyone as long as I am alive."

Everyone stayed silent as the older McQueen spoke. Anna turned to Wooden. "If you cannot get to the tail of this, why don't you ring up the Maestro's girl? I'm not questioning your methods, but isn't getting a better detective the wisest thing to do rather than harassing an old man? " she asked and stormed back into the house.

Wooden sighed deeply and brought out his phone.

Lori was dressing when her phone rang for the second time in five minutes. Unknown to her guardian, her encounter with Axidentol forty-eight hours ago was still affecting her. Her bones appeared to be less strong than they were while there was pain all over her body.

She answered the call and heard the caller introduced himself.

"Yes, Detective Wooden. The mayor already called," she said and dropped the call. She took a deep breath and headed into the workshop.

For years, since Lori could remember, Dr. Maestro always stayed at the workshop far into the night. She found him working when she entered.

"I am trying to modify some of your weapons before it is too late," he began to say.

"Pity we don't have much time. The mayor called again."

Dr. Maestro listened quietly as Lori told her what the mayor said. "How could the cops not know the person behind the missing children?" Dr. Maestro asked.

"They suspected the housekeeper," Lori said.

"Walter?" Dr. Maestro asked, his face showing both surprise and hurt. "I know we humans can be unpredictable. But I cannot imagine Walter hurting anyone, especially not a child."

"Sounds like you know him very well," Lori stated.

"Walter and I grew up together, child," Dr. Maestro said. "He has lived all his life here in Grandstaffville. He married once, but his wife died in childbirth. He didn't remarry. He has served the McQueens for as long as anyone can remember."

"If he isn't behind this, then it must be someone who knows the two affected families."

"But the Grays and the McQueens are enemies. In fact, Alex Gray was the most open critic of Anna McQueen when she was a serving senator," Dr. Maestro said. After what seemed like ages, he spoke again. "Detective Wooden said the clothes the two children wore were left on their beds. He suspected that they were taken naked."

"Naked?" Dr. Maestro asked? He stood there with a blank look on his face, thinking. Then as if by a stroke of luck, he got excited as he started to speak again. "Detective Wooden wouldn't have thought about what I am going to tell you right now, because he was not yet in Grandstaffville when it happened," Dr. Maestro said. "Alex Gray and Anna McQueen may have their differences, but I'm afraid they share a common enemy, Jack the Whisperer. And every villain has his story."

"So, what is this Whisperer's story?" Lori asked.

"When Anna McQueen was still a senator, Jack was accused of being a kid whisperer. It was said he was using some kind of ancient voodoo to sing lullabies to innocent children to lure them in their sleep. Even adults were not safe from his songs. Whether the story was true or false, the thing was that a number of children began to go missing. At the family front, Jack's uncle,

Alex Gray, suddenly retired from NATO to take over the family business. Before he died, Jack's father, Rudolph, had left his share of the family business to his son. Alex Gray lay claims over these shares, which made Jack terribly angry. When this was going on, Anna McQueen suddenly had Jack expelled from the city of Grandstaffville for endangering the lives of children with his voodoo practices. Jack realized that he was wronged by the two families and swore vengeance the day he left Grandstaffville. It's been ten years and no one had seen or heard anything from him."

"If it was Jack the Whisperer, where would I find him?" Lori asked.

"Rudolph had a house behind Orchestra Zoo," Dr. Maestro noted. "If you hadn't seen your father's house for years, it would be the first place you would go when you enter the city. I will bet my life that Jack is there."

"What is with abandoned houses these past few days?" Lori asked.

"Nothing is completely useless, I guess," Dr. Maestro said.

Lori was already gathering her things together as Dr. Maestro spoke. "You should take the police along with you, child."

"There's no time. Call them," Lori said and left the workshop. As soon as she left, Dr. Maestro dialed the Grandstaffville Police Department.

It was exactly as her guardian said. When she arrived at Rudolph's house, she saw from afar that the large family room was dimly lit by candles. Even from outside the house, she could hear a soft melody passing through the winds. She pushed the gate gently and got into the house, where an old Mustang was parked outside, facing the gate.

The closer Lori drew, the harder it became for her to breathe. She moved to the back of the entrance door and removed her earplugs from the bag of gadgets, putting them on. She removed the

Crescendo Ray from the bag and pushed the front door. It was unlocked.

"Are you okay?" she asked immediately when she saw Marvin and Alice. They were on the floor, covered from head to toe with a black linen. There were four candles, two on each side, burning close to them. Jack was nowhere in sight.

"Where is the music coming from?" Lori asked. She looked up. There were probably tens of rooms upstairs from where Jack must be singing his lullaby.

Quickly, she brought the Crescendo Ray in front of her and pulled the trigger with all the strength she could muster. The effort made her body to grow weaker. But it worked. Lori, growing even weaker, watched as Marvin and Alice gradually became conscious.

"The cops are on their way. Run!" she ordered them out of the house and attempted to stand up. Marvin and Alice jumped to their feet and ran out of the house. They did not look back until they were well outside the gate.

Inside the house, Lori, still weakened, heard footsteps descending the stairs. At last, Jack the Whisperer, clapping his hands together, came into full view. He stood before Lori.

"Lori Biscuit," he called mockingly, "the Hero of Grandstaffville. I knew you'd come."

He went over to her and removed her earplugs. "The good ole doctor has cared for you your entire life, hasn't he?" Jack asked. "Tell me, has he ever sang you a song before bedtime?"

Jack did not wait for her answer when he laughed and drew a chair closer. "Now let me sing you a song, child," he said and began to sing a song so calming, it could make even the most stubborn eyes fall asleep.

Lori's eyes began to shut. Jack took her face in his hands, forcing them to stay open. "Look at me! I am Jack the Whisperer," Jack said, taking Lori's bag of gadgets and the black linen from the floor. "Mine will be the last face you'll ever see again. Remember this face."

The last thing that Lori Biscuit remembered was darkness.

When Detective Wooden and his men arrived ten minutes later, the Rudolf Estate was on fire, the old Mustang gone.

CHAPTER SIX

The Wisdom of Kelvin

The Mayor of Grandstaffville ordered the Grandstaffville Police Department to organize a special unit to search for the whereabouts of Jack the Whisperer and Lori. They searched the Orchestra Zoo, the Grandstaffville Library, the Symphony Hall, and all abandoned houses in Grandstaffville. Lori could not be found. They went as far as Marconia, but it was still with the same result. No one had seen Lori or her captor.

At last, the people of Grandstaffville accepted that their beloved hero, Lori Biscuit, had finally met a terrible end in the hands of Jack the Whisperer. For more than a week, the city was in mourning.

Dr. Maestro, who still believed that his beloved Lori was alive somewhere, refused to see anyone who wanted to share his grief.

But he did allow Mark into the house. Every day that Mark made him his special cup of coffee, he would refuse to take it.

On Thursday, the tenth day since Lori's disappearance, the mayor's office and the Grandstaffville Police Department officially declared Lori Biscuit dead and set the date for her funeral service on Saturday at the Grandstaffville Memorial Park.

On the eve of Lori's burial, the men, women and children of the city lit candles outside Dr. Maestro's home on Echo Avenue.

Inside the house, Dr. Maestro sat in a corner of his bedroom with a blank expression on his face. Mark sat in the same room some distance away from him, also silent.

Dr. Maestro, who had never told anyone how he met Lori, suddenly began to speak. He told Mark the story.

Ten years ago, he had gone for an international conference in Plathstonville where some of the world's prominent scientists had gathered to find a cure for the Larengia Virus that had attacked the city. Although the virus had not yet gone beyond Plathstonville, scientists around the world believed that if a cure was not found, it would soon become a global disaster.

One day, Dr. Maestro came out of his hotel room to take a walk around Plathstonville with one of his colleagues. As they moved around the city, he noticed a young child of about four years old following them around. At last, he turned to her. He took a bundle of currency notes from his pockets and gave them to her before he continued his walk. But the girl put the money in the left pocket of her blue pants and went after him. At last, Dr. Maestro turned and asked her where she lived.

"There," she said, pointing at a makeshift tent on the far right of the street.

In Plathstonville, it was easy to find homeless children who had lost their parents to the virus wandering the streets. Some of them were nothing beyond the ages of eight and ten and normally slept at night in makeshift tents on the street. Lori Biscuit, who was wearing a brown hat on her head, was one of them. When Dr. Maestro tried to take it off her head, she held it there forcefully with her palms.

At the end of the conference, he went over to the street where he'd first met her and asked her if she would like to come with him. She nodded and followed him back to Grandstaffville.

"You know, even with her rough hair and unwashed body, she was so sweet and precious. I think she was the most beautiful girl I ever saw in my entire life," Dr Maestro said, as if talking to the wall.

Mark listened, without saying a single word.

"I was supposed to look after her," Dr. Maestro said, the tears gathering in his eyes. "But when she sensed how lonely I was, even at that tender age, she was the one who ended up taking care of me. She knew when I was hurting. She knew what I was thinking. That poor child seemed to know everything."

Mark stood up from his place and went over to the crying old man, hugging him tightly. Dr. Maestro cried without shame. Soon, unable to bear it any longer, Mark, too, let his tears flow freely. They were like that until the early morning of Saturday.

After the church service, where everyone who had known Lori Biscuit and had been touched by her life paid eulogies to her, the entire city of Grandstaffville walked all the way to the Grandstaffville Memorial Park to pay final respects to their hero.

Dr. Maestro, who had aged immensely within the past few days, gave the drawing that Mark made of Lori defeating Fortissimo to represent her corpse.

While all the streets appeared empty, eight-year-old Kelvin was getting his bike out of the garage to go to the funeral, too. Before they left, Andy and Maggie had given him specific orders not to go out of the house no matter what. But Kelvin was one of those children who, when he had set his mind on something, he would not be at peace until he had done exactly that.

He took his bike and pedaled out of the house, until he was right on the edge of Echo Avenue. But instead of going through Alto Avenue where the Grandstaffville Memorial Park was located, he pedaled on through Pitch Avenue, past the City Hall and took a sharp turn as if he was going to Marconia.

Where Kelvin was, in fact, heading was the old Grandstaffville Burial Ground, where the old families of Grandstaffville buried their dead. No one had used the cemetery for the past four years, since the establishment of Grandstaffville Memorial Park. Kelvin had thought that the old burial ground was where Lori was being buried.

When he arrived at the burial ground ten minutes later, he found it empty. No people. No cars.

"Ah!" he exclaimed. "I'm at the wrong place."

But instead of taking his bike and riding away, he parked it behind a tree and began to walk around his new environment fearfully. That was when he saw an old Mustang parked at the exit gate of the cemetery. He started to walk away when he suddenly heard the sound of someone digging.

He stopped and found the closest grave to him, hiding. From there, he watched as a man, who was one of the tallest men he had ever seen, kept digging, completely unaware that he was being watched. He stopped in between his work to sing a lullaby. Kelvin could not hear what he was singing since he was far away from him. But without being told, he knew the man must be Jack the Whisperer.

But where is Lori? he wondered.

He moved away from where he stood and moved closer. That was when he saw a second figure, on the ground and wrapped in a black linen. It was Lori!

Kelvin wanted to go to her. But he knew that he would be of no use to her if he was caught. He carefully went back to his bike and pedaled the distance to Grandstaffville Memorial Park.

Father Anthony Miguel was praying when Kelvin's voice broke through the silence of the graveyards.

"I saw him! I saw him!!" he said, nearly out of breath. He threw his bike on the ground and went straight to Dr. Maestro.

"I saw the tall man. He has Lori."

"Where?" Dr. Maestro asked, becoming full of life. His eyes shone with hope.

"At the graveyards," Kelvin said, to everyone's confusion. "The other one," he added quickly, pointing in the direction he came from.

Dr. Maestro bit his tongue, cursing himself for not thinking too clearly. The Grays, being one of the oldest families in Grandstaffville, had been burying their dead in the Old Grandstaffville Burial Ground for two centuries. The last Gray to be buried there was Rudolph, Jack's father. It became clear to everyone around that Jack took refuge at the cemetery, knowing that everyone would be looking for him.

Detective Wooden was already giving orders to his men to surround every road in Grandstaffville. They did not want to take chances if it came to chasing after the Whisperer in a car.

Andy, Desmond, Anna McQueen, and Alex Gray all got into various cars and headed to the Grandstaffville Burial Ground. Dr. Maestro got into his van with Mark and went back to the workshop to get the new set of modified musical weapons he'd made for Lori.

"For the first time in my life, I'm glad you disobeyed our orders," Maggie said proudly to Kelvin, patting his head. Kelvin disengaged from her and picked up his bike, about to ride after his father.

"Where do you think you are going, young man?" Maggie asked, giving him a stern look.

"Going after Daddy," Kelvin replied.

"Get yourself down from that bike and come home with me right now."

"But I found her!" Kelvin said and quickly sped away from his mother.

When the cops found him, it turned out that Jack the Whisperer was digging up his father's grave. Through his years of his encounters with voodoo, Jack the Whisperer came to believe that by giving a human life in exchange, he could bring his father back to life. That was the only way he could be able to reclaim his inheritance from his uncle, Alex Gray.

When he saw the police, he began to sing in a way that he had never sang before. Gradually, cop after cop dropped to the ground, falling asleep. Andy, struggling not to fail this time around, crawled on the ground towards the villain.

That was when the Crescendo Ray sounded. This made Jack's sound louder and of no effect to anyone. Jack stopped singing, surprised. He looked beside him to make sure that Lori's bag of gadgets was still on the ground. It was. He tried singing again. But the more he sang, the higher the Crescendo Ray soundwaves got.

Dr. Maestro, trailed by Mark, walked towards the villain, still pressing the trigger. It did not take him long to revive the sleeping officers.

Realizing that his lullabies were no longer useful, Jack suddenly took to his heels. His pace was no match for Andy, who had already stood up from the ground.

Mark watched as his father went after Jack the Whisperer with all his might, pushing him against a grave. Jack wailed aloud as his head hit the concrete floor, bloodied.

While this was going on, Lori coughed back to consciousness. She looked around her and saw Mark peering into her face, smiling sheepishly.

"Welcome back," Mark said, taking her hand affectionately.

Lori smiled at him and stood up. Dr. Maestro stood in one spot, disbelieving that his beloved Lori was still alive.

Lori ran to him and hugged him tightly as if her life depended on it. The two began to cry out of happiness. They held each other for what seemed like an eternity until Desmond passed with the handcuffed Jack the Whisperer.

The villain spat at Alex Gray and then glared at Lori. "This is just the beginning, Lori," he said.

"She will be ready for all of you," a small voice said to him.

Mark knew that mischievous voice.

"When did you get here, you little rascal?" he asked Kelvin, who was already holding Lori's hands.

"Just now," Kelvin said and cocked his head to one side. "What did I miss?"

Everyone laughed as they left the cemetery.

***

Down in the city, the mayor, who had already received information that Lori was alive, invited the people to the City Hall for a music festival to celebrate their returning hero.

But deep within his mind, Dr. Maestro was worried. He had been thinking of what Jack the Whisperer meant when he said, "This is just the beginning."

He decided to dismiss the thought from his mind. He raised his head to see a smiling Lori waving him to come into the car. He did, silently praying that whatever it was that was coming, his beloved Lori would survive it. And he would make sure she did.

He would not fail her again.

CHAPTER SEVEN

The Return of Fortissimo

A month after the arrest of Jack the Whisperer, the city of Grandstaffville was in peace. As things became normal, Bar Line Park and City Hall were filled with people every weekend.

It was as if the city had never witnessed terrible things within the past few weeks.

At Dr. Maestro's house on Echo Avenue, Mark, Andrew and Lori Biscuit continued to enjoy each other's friendship.

Dr. Maestro had encouraged her to take as much rest as possible. "You can only save others when you have enough strength to save yourself first," he had said to her one day.

And Lori listened to his advice. She began to do something she had not done in a long time, walk around Grandstaffville for leisure. Mark was always with her.

They walked across every major street in Grandstaffville. Sometimes, the mischievous Kelvin followed them on his bike, stopping at the point they stopped and continuing from where they continued. He was totally unaware they knew he was following them. Whenever he got tired, he would pedal his bike back home to Echo Avenue. By so doing, Kelvin came to know nearly all the major places in Grandstaffville, more than anyone his age.

"Hope you know that little rascal has been following us?" Mark said.

"I know. Let him be, Mark," replied Lori. "He's okay as long as we know he's following us."

Everywhere they went during their walks, people stared at Lori. Mark knew she was popular in Grandstaffville.

But she was one of those people who rarely socialized like the rest of the people in Grandstaffville. Because of that, not everyone got to see her. Sometimes, whenever she saved the city from a villain, she would call for celebration, reinforcing her mantra, "Eat healthy and be merry. No one knows what tomorrow brings."'

But as soon as the celebration was over, Lori would disappear from public view, back to her underground workshop, back to her guardian, Dr. Maestro.

As they walked, some of the women came out of their houses to thank her for all she was doing for the city. A group of children playing on the field suddenly stopped and stared at her. At last, the youngest of them shouted her name. Lori smiled and waved at him.

"Who would have thought that one day you'd be more popular than the Lanes twins?" Mark asked, smiling broadly at her.

The Lanes twins he was referring to were the girl, Ivy, and the boy, Jeremy Lanes. They were famous for not only their perfect physical resemblance and enviable beauty, but also for their similar mannerisms.

Complete opposites of their parents, Martha and Patrick Lane, the twins were not always comfortable in public. Instead, it was easier to find them alone together, enjoying each other's company. Everyone in Grandstaffville knew the Lanes twins. Every evening, they would come out of the Lanes' Estate on Alto Avenue and head for the Molto River. It was like a ritual they never failed to observe. No one knew what exactly the twins were looking for every time at the river. But it helped to fuel the rumors that they were not really humans but spirit beings who would one day destroy Grandstaffville.

The rumors made most parents keep their children away from Ivy and Jeremy. Whether the twins were troubled by the rumors, no one could say. But each time they passed by and someone looked at them, they would turn and smile back at the person and continue their walk.

"What's wrong with always going to River Molto? People are always uncomfortable with things they don't understand," Dr. Maestro told Lori one day when she asked about the Lanes twins. "Those are just some innocent kids in love with nature. That's all."

But not all of Grandstaffville thought unkindly of the twins. Those who were friends with Martha and Patrick swore that Ivy and Jeremy were some of the nicest and respectful kids in the whole of Grandstaffville.

"Who would have thought people would know my name as they do Ivy and Patrick's?" Lori rephrased Mark's question.

She remembered the first time she came to Grandstaffville and the hostility of the people towards her. But everything had changed now.

Mark turned to her and squeezed her hand. Even without being told, he knew what she was thinking. "We have been walking around for hours now," he said when they had reached Trent's Farms, which belonged to the dairy farmer, Stephen Trent. Kelvin had turned back to the city about ten minutes ago.

"Yes," Lori agreed. "We should go back now."

They had not taken more than a few steps towards home when they heard a *Boom!!!* The sound was repetitive in the air.

"We have to get back right now!" Lori shouted and began to run as fast as she could.

"Who do you think it is right now?" Mark asked when he caught up with her. Although he did not say it, he was surprised to see her outrun him. But that was Lori—always full of surprises.

"I can't say!" she shouted into the wind. "Maybe someone new."

As they drew closer to the city, they saw people running from the direction of the Melody Museum. They were running away from the Collectors.

The Collectors were the goons who accompanied Fortissimo whenever he wanted to unleash disaster on Grandstaffville. The last time Lori faced him, he did not come with them. As soon as she saw the Collectors, she looked around for their leader. She did not see any sign of him.

"I wonder where he is," she said to no one in particular.

Marked looked at her. "I thought the last time you turned Fortissimo into a very soft Pianissimo, you told the mayor to keep him safe in the Orchestra Zoo?" he asked her.

"Dr. Maestro has been suspecting for a long time that someone is releasing the animals from the zoo. I'm beginning to think the same thing, too," Lori said.

A group of students ran past them. They were followed by the Collectors, who were jumping and falling on the ground, causing minor tremors as they did so.

"What in God's precious name are they doing here on Saturday?" Lori asked.

"Who?" Mark asked, confused.

"The students."

"My mum told my dad they are expecting the Grandstaffville High School Students today," Mark replied.

"This means someone knew about this and set the animals at the zoo free," Lori reasoned. "Look, there's nothing I can do without my bag of gadgets."

"I will rush over to your house and get them for you," Mark offered. "After all, I'm the better runner."

"Not anymore," Lori said and sprinted out of his sight. Three minutes later, she was in the underground workshop.

"I was beginning to worry," her guardian said when he saw her. "Well, who's our visitor this time around?"

"The Collectors," Lori replied.

"This means Fortissimo is—" Dr. Maestro began to say.

"Out of the Orchestra Zoo," Lori completed.

Dr. Maestro sighed. Every day, something new happened to confirm his suspicions.

"Here," he said, pointing at Lori's new bag of gadgets. "Every weapon there is remodeled. Come, let's see what you can do with this." He removed Decrescendo Ray and gave it to Lori.

Lori collected it and was about to shoot when she heard, "Wait." She turned to see her guardian rushing to the sound system in the workshop. He turned up the volume and signaled her to shoot the ray.

She did.

The ray completely drowned the music as if there was not a single sound in the workshop.

"This is a sure thing!" she exclaimed.

"We just need to make sure you're keeping your energy up," Dr. Maestro advised, signs of worry on his face. "Did Mark tell you what happened to him the last time he used the Accelerando Whip on Larghissimo?"

"No," Lori answered. "What happened?"

"Well, he was in bed for two days, completely weak from head to toe."

"That explains why I didn't see him for two days. But why?"

Dr. Maestro walked over to her and took her hands. "There's a reason only you and I can control any of the musical weapons, child. They are not for everybody to use," he said. "If they are, I wouldn't have spent a decade training you on how to use them. Enough talk. You have to go out now."

Lori quickly embraced him and dashed out of the workshop. Just as she reached the Museum where a large number of students and other visitors were trapped, Fortissimo chose that same moment to announce his presence.

"Hello, Grandstaffville! Miss me?" His deep voice tore through their ears like a knife razor cutting through flesh.

A boy suddenly ran out through the museum door. Fortissimo saw him and screamed in his direction. The sound lifted the boy high into the air and landed him on the ground, at Lori's feet.

"Yeah, that's right," the villain said when he saw Lori. "How are you enjoying my show, Lori Biscuit?" he asked, a big grin on his face.

"Nothing spectacular," Lori shouted at the top of the roof of the museum where he stood.

"Soldiers," Fortissimo called. At once, all the Collectors stopped, facing the roof. "She said your show is not interesting. Formation!"

The Collectors quickly formed a line, awaiting instructions.

"Attack!" Fortissimo's voice commanded.

Lori already knew what she needed to do. She waited until all the people had run out of immediate harm before she turned to the villain. "Come get me yourself!"

"With pleasure!" Fortissimo laughed and lifted himself high into the air, higher than Lori imagined he ever could. She continued to watch him until he disappeared totally from sight.

She was about to head for the army of Collectors destroying everyone on sight when she heard someone cry out her name, "Lori!"

It was Kelvin.

How long has he been here? Lori wondered.

"Kelvin, run home!" she screamed at him.

But Kelvin did not move. Instead, he kept pointing at the sky. Lori looked up and saw nothing.

"I say, go h..." she began to say again when she heard the sound of something falling in from the sky at high speed. Fortissimo!

She did not waste time. She withdrew her modified Decrescendo Ray and pulled the trigger with all her might then held her breath, waiting. She did not have to wait for long.

Fortissimo, changing form slowly, appeared in full view. "I will come again and again," he said as he transformed into a Pianissimo.

There was silence everywhere. The Collectors had all turned to Pianississimo, smaller versions of their master.

"Entertaining!" Kelvin said.

Someone smacked him from the back. It was Mark.

"Have you no business than to always be in the wrong place all the time?" he asked.

"No, I haven't."

Mark ignored him.

"They aren't bad, are they?" he said to Lori, pointing at the destroyed buildings.

"I've seen a lot worse," she answered. "I need to wait here and see that Fortissimo is properly kept safe."

"Well, let me take this young rascal home," Mark said and held Kelvin by the hand.

Lori remembered what Dr. Maestro told her at the workshop.

"Hey, Mark," Lori called.

"Yes."

"Thanks again for that day with Larghissimo. Dr. Maestro told me what happened to you after that."

"Nothing much," Mark said, smiling. "That's pretty much what you do for friends."

Lori nodded and watched as he walked away with Kelvin.

CHAPTER EIGHT

Every City Has Its Rogues

For two weeks, sixteen-year-old Jeremy Lanes had been having nightmares. In the dreams, a strange darkness was strangling him and Ivy, followed by the terrifying voice of a man dressed in black. Immediately after this particular dream, a new one would begin. In it, he woke up one day, side by side with his twin sister in a forest far from home. Neither of them could remember who they were, where they were, and who their family was.

The first time the dreams started, Jeremy told no one and simply dismissed them. But when they kept recurring, he knew he had no other choice.

"I am having the same dreams," Ivy confided in him the day he told her.

"But what do they mean?" he asked, confused.

If anything, the Lanes twins were not new to dreams. In fact, they had dreamed dreams as much as the desert had had its fair share of sand dust.

On this particular night, Ivy dreamed that she was tied with a thick rope from her toes, until she died of starvation. When she tried to get free, black blood began to leak from her nose, down to her knees, staining her. When she tried to scream, she realized that the darkness had taken her voice.

Troubled by her dream, she woke up from the bed. She sat completely quietly on it, as a corpse placed inside a coffin. She remained that way until the first light of dawn when she walked out of her room and went straight to Jeremy's room. He was expecting her.

As soon as she opened the door, she walked into the room and began to cry. "Do you think we are in trouble?" she asked, sniffing.

Jeremy walked up to her and hugged her. "Maybe," he said softly. "I can't think clearly. I feel like I need fresh air to clear my head. It appears too heavy for me."

"Mine, too," Ivy confessed.

"Should we go to the river?" he suggested.

"Isn't it too early?" Ivy asked, genuinely concerned.

Jeremy did not answer her. Instead, he sauntered to his closet, and within two minutes, he was fully dressed. Seeing that he was serious, Ivy ran down to her room and quickly put her clothes on and went after him.

As the twins walked out of the house, it was as if a strange force was calling forth to them, to their deaths.

That morning, as Ivy and Jeremy headed towards River Molto, Lori also could not sleep back at her place. Since her last encounter with Fortissimo, she had begun to survive each night thinking of the best possible way to fight the villains when they returned to the city of Grandstaffville. Right now, she stood up from the bed and began to pace her room.

During her last encounter with Fortissimo, he promised her he would return to Grandstaffville, repeatedly. She knew these were not ordinary words of a monster refusing to accept the defeat. No. If anything, they were too daring to be ordinary.

So far, so good. She had become so familiar with fighting villains that the possibility of them coming back had never crossed her mind.

Outside her room, she could hear the chorale of birds, welcoming the morning. Through her window, her vision caught a particular bird perched on the enormous trunk of a tree, moving its head in every direction. The other birds, as if sensing the intrusion, suddenly went quiet, making the area grow hushed. It was as if they held their breath for something coming.

Lori watched the bird intently until it turned and faced her direction. She sighed and moved away from the window and headed out of her room.

She found Dr. Maestro at the workshop. She pushed the door slightly and stepped in.

"You're up early today," he said when she greeted him.

A quick, wide smile flashed on her face before she spoke. "I've not being sleeping much these days."

Dr. Maestro dropped the sledgehammer he was holding on a table and sat down on a chair. This was what Lori loved about him. Whenever she was desperate to tell him something, he would drop whatever it was he was doing and then give her the attention she hungered for.

The old man watched her, smiling, expecting her to tell him what was wrong. Instead, Lori did not speak again. But he could see the way her chest was rising. He knew this to be an indication that a great fear had overtaken her.

Lori drew closer to him, as if she was moving away from the shadows around her. "We need to come up with a plan to rid Grandstaffville of monsters," she said.

Even though she was standing closer to him, Dr. Maestro felt as if it was the farthest she had ever been from him. It was her voice. As she spoke, he could have sworn that her voice was almost impossible to hear.

He opened his mouth again to ask her if she was all right. A second before he could do so, Lori's body froze as she backed away from him, slowly, and then collapsed on the ground.

Immediately, Dr. Maestro rushed to her, confirmed that she was breathing, and then he gently raised her legs above her heart level. His mind troubled, he untied her belt and removed her collars.

A minute later, Lori regained consciousness and attempted to get up quickly.

"No," Dr. Maestro said. "Stay down. Relax your body. You've not been getting enough rest."

"This is why we need to come up with a plan to put the villains away for all time. And then I could rest," she said, lying back in Dr. Maestro's arms.

After what seemed like eternity, he helped her get up and then led her back into her room.

"Why aren't you saying anything yet?" Lori asked, staring into his eyes. She knew he cared deeply for her and that he would do anything within his powers to make sure that no harm came to her.

But Lori was not, in reality, worried about herself. She was desperate to find a final solution to the recent happenings in Grandstaffville so that he, too, could find peace. She was aware of the look in his eyes whenever she returned from any of her encounters with one villain or the other. She knew the words in that look and what they meant.

Dr. Maestro's breathing thinned as he spoke. "I was afraid I had lost you," he confessed, coming face to face with her. "The first day I saw you and agreed to look after you, I promised myself that no harm would ever come to you under my care. I intend to keep that promise. Now, rest," he said and turned back towards the door.

As he left, Lori closed her eyes and went into a deep sleep, one like she had not had in a long time. When she woke up hours later, she walked back to the studio and found the old man talking on the phone. He dropped the call as soon as he saw Lori at the door.

"What is it?" she asked, looking at him.

He knew there was no way he could lie to her. Lori could read him more than anyone could, as if she was his second mind. He watched as she leaned her weight against the door, smiling broadly at him. He sighed. "It's the Lanes twins, Ivy and Jeremy," he said.

"What happened to them?" Lori asked. Her smile disappeared from her face, replaced by lines of concerns. Although the Lanes twins always kept to themselves, she had always felt a certain likeness for Ivy and her brother.

"Mr. Lanes called the police to report that they left home as soon as it was morning. When they did not return, he feared that something bad had happened to them. The police have combed through the entire Grandstaffville area without finding either of them." Dr. Maestro's eyes followed Lori as he spoke. He knew what she was going to do.

And she did just that! She retreated into her room, and three minutes later, she was heading out of the workshop. "I'm going after them," she said, then took her bag of gadgets and left.

As she reached the end of Echo Avenue, her mind was running through many possibilities of where Ivy and Jeremy might have gone. The first place that came to her mind, of course, was River Molto. She headed in that direction.

By the time she reached the river, it was already an hour to noon. She looked around, looking for any sign that would tell her where they were.

That was when an old woman, looking to be in her late seventies, approached her. "I saw the Lanes kids," she said to Lori.

"They were here?" Lori asked and quickly wished she had not asked that. Of course, they were here. That was why she came here first, wasn't?

"I saw them with him," the woman said, her voice almost like a whisper.

"With who?" Lori asked, curious.

Dr. Maestro once told her about Celina Kyle, a widow who also lost her only child during the tragic fire that broke out in Grandstaffville a year before her arrival. Since then, Celina retreated from the public. She could always be found at the River Molto, claiming that she was waiting for her son.

"The people think I've gone crazy. I hear the things they say about me," Celina continued. "But I know things. Many things, girl." She stopped speaking and seemed to forget what she was saying before she went on again.

"The Lanes kids. They're the reason you're here, aren't they? Well, I saw him. He took them. Never seen a fierce-looking man like him, always in and out of prison," the old woman said and spat on the ground to show her disgust.

Lori was more than curious now. "Who are you talking about?" she asked.

"Timbre, girl. Timbre. That's what he calls himself. His name is Richard. He used to be a sweet boy. He was my baby's best friend. One day he woke up and decided he wanted to be a bandit. He succeeded. He's a shape shifter. He changes all the time. By the time you notice that it's him, the dirty man can steal anything, switch anything, and forge anything, including your eyes if you're not careful. He was here, thirty minutes after the kids came. Seems like he has broken into the Orchestra Zoo. Saw him with many animals. I hid as soon as I saw them. But not the poor kids. Do you know they're always here at the river to keep me company?" Celina asked, her face beaming with sadness at the memory. "Who freed him from the prisons, anyway?" she asked.

Lori ignored her question. "Where do you think he's headed?" Lori asked.

"There," Celina pointed north, "Opera town."

Lori thanked the old woman and left immediately. As she went, she messaged Dr. Maestro to tell Andy to meet her in Opera Town.

Opera town was two kilometers away from Grandstaffville. When Lori got there, it did not take long to find Ivy and Jeremy in Timpani forest, tied with a thick rope against a tree. As Lori drew closer to them, she saw a bow and arrow on the ground and then everything became clear to her. They were set against the tree like a shooting target for their captor.

Lori looked around, wondering where Timbre was. She saw no one in sight. When she went on her knees, about to loosen the ropes, a voice asked warily, "Who are you?" It was Ivy's.

Lori was shocked. She had met the twins numerous times. They knew her. They knew who she was. Why, then, was Ivy asking her who she was? Something was wrong, but Lori decided to find out later.

"I'm Lori," she introduced herself. "I'm from Grandstaffville. Your parents are worried about you."

"Grandstaffville? Where's that? Are we from there?" Jeremy asked.

"We have parents?" Ivy asked also.

Lori sighed. *Memory loss.*

She remembered one of the many stories that Dr. Maestro told her about how some of the animals in the Orchestra Zoo could cause memory loss when the sounds they made were manipulated. She remembered Cecilia saying she saw Timbre with many animals. According to Dr. Maestro, the victim remained in that state even after the animals had left. Only by using the sound bender, would they be able to recover.

She quickly retrieved it from her bag of gadgets. She looked around and when she was sure no one else was inside, she blew it with all her strength. After she stopped blowing and waited for her breath to turn to normal, she heard a voice behind her.

"Lori? What are you... What are we doing here?" Jeremy asked. He turned to his right and saw Ivy also tied to a tree. Furious, he began to squirm his body, attempting to free himself. Lori went over to him and untied the rope. Jeremy dashed to his sister as soon as he could and untied the rope holding her. Lori watched as the twins hugged each other.

"Our dreams were true," Ivy said.

"Thank you for coming to save us," Jeremy said. "Where are we, and how did you find us?"

"I went to River Molto and Cecilia told me she saw when Timbre took you."

By now, the three had begun to walk through the woods, back to Grandstaffville. As they did, Jeremy was quietly watching the ground, in the way that a skilled tracker did. "And now he's going back to Grandstaffville," he declared.

"Timbre? How did you know?" Lori asked, shocked.

Jeremy pointed to the ground. There were prints of gumboot in the wet soil. "I've been tracing these footprints," he said.

"He knew you'd come after us," Ivy reasoned. "Now that he's going back to Grandstaffville, he did not want you to be there."

Lori began to panic. If Timbre had freed the animals from the Orchestra Zoo, then he had played them all by succeeding in luring her away from Grandstaffville to achieve his grand plans. Before she knew it, she had begun to run. Ivy and Jeremy followed suit.

They had barely gone past the last junction that separated Grandstaffville from Opera Town when they saw Andy's car speeding towards them.

"We are doomed, Lori," he said as soon as he stopped the car. His T-shirt was ripped all over, as if he had just walked through barbwires. "This is the end of Grandstaffville!" he lamented.

Lori and the twins got into the car and Andy reversed it, toward Grandstaffville. Lori sat opposite him, silent, and lost in thoughts. After her encounter with Jack the Whisperer, Kelvin had once promised the villain that she would be ready for them when the time came.

At last, she closed her eyes and said a silent prayer in her heart.

If this was the end, she hoped for the strength to not only save Grandstaffville but also the old man who gave her a new life.

CHAPTER NINE

The Road to War

For the rest of her life, Lori would remember what she saw as soon as Andy drove into Grandstaffville. For hundreds of times, she wanted to tell herself that all that she was seeing was a mere dream. But as the car continued to cut through the city, everything that was once beautiful and peaceful in it gave way to total chaos.

Every villain she had ever fought since the day Dr. Maestro turned her into the Musical Detective was on the street, appearing more powerful and vengeful than they had ever been.

A young girl of nine ran through the street, shouting her mother's name. One of the Collectors, Fortissimo's goons, went after her. Lori quickly brought out her Decrescendo Ray to soften the Collector when she heard a woman screaming through the wind. Axidentol had picked her up from the ground.

Lori, still dazed, went after him. The moment she took a step, another voice stopped her in her tracks.

"Grandstaffville," Jack the Whisperer shouted as he rode into the city in his old Mustang. "I bring you flowers!" he added, spreading his arms to indicate the villains at work.

The instant that Desmond, who was rushing to keep a boy out of harm's way, heard Jack's voice, he dropped the boy on the ground and geared up to attack the Whisperer.

The Whisperer chose that moment to sing. His soft voice gently tore through Desmond's body until he dropped to the ground. By the time Desmond closed his eyes, the Whisperer, watching him, stopped singing. He took up a bundle of flowers from the passenger seat and came down from his car. He drew closer to Desmond, spat on him, and then began to pluck each of them out, dropping them on the fallen man.

"Smell the taste of my master's victory over your beloved Grandstaffville," he said in his gentle voice, laughing wickedly.

Lori watched in horror at what she was seeing from where she stood. Dr. Maestro's worst fear was here. A few years ago, he had told her he feared that, someday, a terrible thing would happen to Grandstaffville and there would be nothing anyone could do about it.

Lori looked around to see if she could see any other familiar faces. Andy had taken Ivy and Jeremy home. They appeared physically weakened by their last ordeal. She wondered where her guardian was and what he was doing at this moment.

Jack the Whisperer raised his eyes and met Lori's. "Ah, Lori," he said, his lips curled into a mocked smile. "I want you to meet my new friends," he added, pointing up.

Out of curiosity, anger, and hatred for the Whisperer, Lori looked up. Immediately, the Cymbals, two of the most dangerous animals in the Orchestra Zoo, screamed from up above the tower of the Symphony Hall. The sound tossed Lori and the men and women near it to the ground.

Lori was surprised when she regained control of herself. In all her life in Grandstaffville, she had only heard of the Cymbals. If anything, no child below the age of sixteen had ever seen them. In fact, for most people in the city, the Cymbals were simply legendary creatures. It was said that they made the most dangerous sound of all the animals and that whenever they lifted high into the air, they could cause an earthquake twice as large as one Fortissimo was capable of.

Lori began to sweat. For the first time in many years, she felt terrified. Around her, people were running through the streets of the city, hiding from the villains. The Collectors were having a field day. As they chased after the people, they laughed like little children in the playground playing with colors.

Lori saw a mother holding a baby in her arms speed past her, a dog following closely behind them. The dog stopped and turned to bark at an approaching Collector. The woman stopped and shouted the dog's name. It was too late. The attacking Collector screamed and hurled the dog out of its way. The dog whimpered and slouched on the ground. His owner took one last look at him before she resumed running.

Lori thought of Dr. Maestro again. It was obvious now to her that someone had released all the animals on Grandstaffville. But who had such power? The mayor?

No! Lori quickly dismissed the thought from her mind.

Although the mayor did not always see eye to eye with some of the people, he had proved to them that he only dreamed the best for the city. Wasn't he the first person to call her whenever something bad was happening to Grandstaffville?

Lori looked at her bag of gadgets. She knew that with all the villains out on the streets, there was no weapon in the bag to fight all of them. She needed help. Moreover, who was in the best position to help her than the man who made her who she was today?

She took one last look at the Whisperer, turned, and ran homeward. As she ran through the city, until she reached Echo Avenue, the scenes she saw changed from one form of horror to another. Houses were sliced in two as if they were loaves of bread. She immediately knew which villain was capable of such levels of destruction. *Fortissimo!* she cursed under her breath. She wondered what Fortissimo was doing on Echo Avenue.

Three minutes later, she was home. When she walked into the underground workshop, she found her guardian sitting on a chair, his hands cuffed.

"Sometimes, I would always look out at the evening sky and wonder what I could make of this city," Lori heard a familiar voice saying. "Power is everything," the voice continued speaking.

"What you're thinking of doing will destroy us all," Dr. Maestro said, refusing to look up as he spoke.

"Well, then, I have no choice but to destroy the whole city and rebuild it from the scratch. But not until I have gotten rid of interfering people like you."

Lori listened as the owner of the voice laughed.

"Do you know that no matter what I do for the city, the people always think you're doing more for them? They call you *The Kind Doctor*! They think you saved them all by bringing in that little rat who doesn't know her place. As long as I'm in this city, there's no place for her," the voice said and spat on the ground furiously. The voice softened and spoke as persuasively. "But I could spare her if only you give me the Baton."

Lori's ear trembled at the mention of the Baton. She remembered Dr. Maestro telling her that it was the most powerful musical weapon in the world. No animal could withstand its power.

Why would someone need the Baton? she wondered. If anyone else had it, it only meant that the person would become the most powerful person in Grandstaffville, or even in the world.

Dr. Maestro raised his eyes slowly and looked at his torturer. "I cannot give you what you seek," he said, his voice tired. "I don't have it."

"Liar!" the voice said angrily. "You were believed to be the possessor of the Baton. It has been with you for the last fifty years. I need it right now, old man!"

"I told you I don't have it," Dr. Maestro insisted. "And even if I do, I will not give it to you. I've seen what power in the wrong hands can do. It destroyed your grandfather. And I should have known it was you who was freeing the villains all along. But how could I press charges against Grandstaffville's number one man without any evidence? How?" Dr. Maestro asked, looking sadly at the wall, before he continued. "And as for Lori, she belongs here in Grandstaffville as much as anyone else. She became my daughter the day I agreed to take charge of her. Except, you kill me, no one touches her. I will make sure of that until my last breath."

When Lori heard her what guardian said, she could not stop the tears from gathering in her eyes.

"Well, then, you leave me with no choice," the owner of the voice said. "You know one thing I love about myself, Maestro?"

Dr. Maestro stared at the man, silently.

The man continued speaking, nevertheless. "I always get what I want. I promise you I will run this city down if you don't give me that. Before your very eyes, Grandstaffville will fall. The City Hall, the Orchestra Zoo, the Symphony Hall, the Bar Line Park and every place worthy of history in this city shall bow down to the fire that I shall ignite."

"God have mercy on you," Dr. Maestro said, still looking downwards.

Lori moved silently away from the door and looked into the room where the interrogation was ongoing. Right before her eyes, she saw the mayor pacing over her guardian. And everything fell into place.

CHAPTER 10

The Arrival of Peace

Lori was stuck to the ground when she saw the mayor's face. Everything became clear to her now. He knew she, alone, would be able to stop him. To get rid of her, he had been setting her in the way of danger in a way that she would not be able to survive.

Watching him through her hidden spot, she decided to tiptoe to him and knock him unconscious. But just as she took her first step from the door, she heard another movement. It was Fortissimo.

"Listen to me," the mayor said to Dr. Maestro. "You don't need to prove this stubborn and risk Lori's life. What do you have to lose? Just give me what I came for!"

"I have everything to lose," Dr. Maestro said.

"Like what?" the mayor asked, bringing his face to stare at the old man.

"Integrity," Dr. Maestro said, his eyes wet. "A man without integrity is as good as dead. Some men can live without that. I'm not one of them."

"Then, let me see if integrity can keep you safe from Fortissimo," the man said.

The mayor then clicked his hand and Fortissimo came into full view. He faced in the direction of Dr. Maestro and breathed out. His breath pushed the old man, still tied to his chair, against the wall. As soon as his body hit the underground wall, Dr. Maestro gasped in pain and then quickly turned around, facing the mayor.

"Is that all you can do?" he asked with a mock smile on his face.

"Oh, no! No!" the mayor said, shaking his hand. "I've just begun."

Even as he spoke, he was confused within himself. He was happy that, at last, he finally had the widely loved and respected Dr. Maestro at his mercy. It was what he had always wanted. But he was also sad that the old man was not as soft as he had expected him to be, even when he was face-to-face with Fortissimo. The mayor looked at his watch and stood up, turning to Fortissimo. "Keep your eyes on him. I will rummage around his private room and see if I could find the Baton." He patted Dr. Maestro's head and left the workshop.

Lori did not move from where she stood. Instead, she was careful enough to remain unnoticed. She promised herself she was not going anywhere until she was sure that no harm would come to her guardian.

Five minutes later, the mayor emerged from Dr. Maestro's room.

"Well, I couldn't find anything," he said to no one in particular. "But be careful, old man. I'm not leaving here without the Baton. Your little rat is busy on the streets. She's not coming here anytime soon.

Lori knew there was no way she would be able to save both Dr. Maestro and Grandstaffville without help. But who should she go to for help? At last, she smiled and retreated out of the workshop.

She knew just the right people to form an immediate army. The instant she came into the streets, the Collectors were everywhere. She continued to run until she got to Mark's house.

Andy, who saw her coming through the window, was waiting for her at the door.

Lori breathed deeply when she got into the house. Mark rushed over to her and hugged her. Kelvin was lying calmly on the sofa, sleeping.

"The mayor has captured Dr. Maestro," Lori said at once. "He wants the Baton."

"The Baton?" Andy and Maggie chorused.

"Yes. Dr. Maestro once told me the Baton is the most powerful weapon in the world. And from what I gathered at the workshop, he's been its custodian for fifty years now."

"I've always known there was something fishy about the mayor," Andy said. "What do you want us to do?"

"I want you to get ready for me when I return. The Collectors and the other villains are all over the city. I have to save Dr. Maestro first. After that, I will need you to drive me to the Symphony Hall to end this permanently."

When Lori finished speaking, she found Mark was no longer in the room. Andy and Maggie noticed, too. Kelvin was still sleeping on the sofa.

"Where did that boy go just now?" Andy asked.

"Mark?" Maggie called, looking upstairs. "Are you in your room, honey?"

"How could he go up without us knowing?" Andy asked.

There was silence.

"It's okay," Lori said and went for the exit door.

As soon as she opened the door, she saw Mark smiling at her, broadly. He was not alone.

Ivy, Jeremy, Alice, Lola, and Marvin were all standing before her, smiling, too.

"We have come to do what we can for the city," Jeremy said. "We are going to unite with you, Lori Biscuit."

Lori came down from the porch where she was standing and hugged them as they laughed together.

"You people look like some little Freedom Fighters," Maggie said, smiling at the kids.

"Well, wait for our victory," Mark said as they all went back into the streets.

"How many of them do you think are out there?" Lola asked on the way.

"About a hundred? Or more," Jeremy said.

"Don't worry, guys," Lori comforted. "We'll be just fine. At least, we've got one another."

"I can't believe I'm going to fight villains!" Marvin exclaimed.

"Not now, first, we have to save Dr. Maestro," Lori said just as the six of them approached Dr. Maestro's house.

"What's the plan, Lori?" Jeremy asked.

Lori stopped. She actually had not thought of any plan. Of course, they wouldn't just arrive on the scene and the mayor would surrender all of a sudden.

"We should cause a distraction and make the mayor send out Fortissimo," Mark suggested.

"Perfect!" Lori accepted. "Once he comes out, then I will use the Decrescendo Ray on him."

They had not finished speaking when Ivy left them and went over to the door leading directly into the underground workshop. She hit the door and ran out of sight.

"Who's there?" Lori and her friends heard the mayor shout from within.

Meanwhile, inside the workshop, the mayor, in a sudden fit of anger, swept his hands through the table containing some of Dr. Maestro's recent experiments. Some of the glass objects fell on the ground and broke into pieces.

"Respect science, you dimwit!" Dr. Maestro shouted at him.

"Enough!" the mayor shouted back. "I have had enough words coming out of your stinking mouth. One more word from you and I will make sure I bury you under this underground."

"You think I'm afraid of men like you? I've seen worse," Dr. Maestro said.

"Well, you haven't seen death, have you?" the mayor asked. Without waiting for an answer, he snapped his fingers at Fortissimo. "Finish him," he ordered, taking the briefcase he came with.

Fortissimo opened his mouth wide, going in for the kill.

Another loud bang came on the door.

"Who's there?" The mayor spun around sharply. "Fortissimo, go check and see who that is. And, show no mercy!"

That was just what Lori needed. She quickly brought out her Decrescendo Ray and waited for Fortissimo. She was getting ready to bring the weapon out in front of her, when she noticed Ivy was still beside the door.

"Ivy, move away from the door," she screamed.

It was too late.

From inside the workshop, as he approached, Fortissimo breathed out, forcefully peeling the door out of the way. Before Lori could say anything, she saw Jeremy rushing over to his twin sister, who was already bleeding on her right hand.

She was so taken by the sight that she did not know when Fortissimo began to come for her.

"Hey!" a voice shouted.

Lori swiftly turned around and saw Kelvin on his bike, rapidly pedaling away as Fortissimo went after him. Immediately, she knew what had happened. The monster was about to shut her down when Kelvin distracted him, saving her.

She gasped in horror and ran as fast as she could after Fortissimo, and when she got few inches away from him, she pulled the trigger of the Crescendo Ray with all her might.

Fortissimo, who was just about to pounce on Kelvin, groaned heavily, and then began to shrink slowly, until he completely crashed on the ground.

Kelvin instantly reversed his bike and rode towards Lori. When he reached her, she hugged him firmly. "It seems you're created to be saving me all the time," she said, smiling. She raised her head and looked at Kelvin. "I thought you were sleeping when I was at your house?"

"Turned out I wasn't," Kelvin said, a mischievous smile taking over his face.

"Hey, Lori," Dr. Maestro called.

Lori twirled her body in the direction of his voice.

She clasped her palms to her mouth, unable to believe what she was seeing. She ran into her guardian's arms, staying in his warmth for what seemed like an eternity.

"I need the Baton," she said, when they disengaged. "This is the time."

"You're right; this is the time," Dr. Maestro said, walking back into the workshop.

When she got inside, Lori found the mayor in the chair where he had initially strapped Dr. Maestro.

"How did you do this?" she asked Mark, who was standing guard over him.

"It's easy to knock him out," Mark replied, smiling. "He talks too much."

They were still talking when they heard the sounds of cars outside. A few seconds later, Andy, Anna McQueen, and Alex Gray entered the underground workshop.

Dr. Maestro said nothing. Instead, he went into his room and then returned. Everyone watched him, curious.

"It is time to explore the power of the Baton, child," he said, handing it over to Lori.

Lori took it and winked at Andy.

He understood. He looked at Kelvin who was standing by the door. "Stay here," he instructed.

"I will," Kelvin replied, a mischievous smile taking over his face again.

"I know that look," Andy said, trying to sound serious.

"Okay," Kelvin accepted defeat. "I'm staying with the doctor."

Dr. Maestro looked at the boy, smiling in a way he did whenever he noticed something special about anyone.

Together with Lori, Andy left the workshop, heading for his car. Outside, Jeremy, Alice, Marvin, and Lola were waiting for them. On seeing them, Andy sighed and opened the back door. They drove down quietly to the Symphony Hall.

As they drove through the city, the streets were silent like a graveyard, except for the army of Collectors, who began to return to the Symphony. Their steps on the ground made the earth tremble.

"Fast!" Lori instructed.

"I'm trying!" Andy replied, speeding up.

At last, they got to the Symphony Hall.

"Take this," Lori said, giving the Crescendo Ray to Andy when she saw Jack the Whisperer singing his lullabies. Next to him, Desmond was on the ground, motionless.

"Dada!" Lola shouted when she saw her father on the ground. Jeremy held her by the hand.

"I want you to shoot this," Lori said to Andy as she got out of the car. Then she began to give instructions to Jeremy, Alice, and Marvin.

"I want you to help me distract the Collectors, until I've climbed up to the roof of the Symphony Hall.

"Okay!" Jeremy, Alice, and Marvin chorused.

Lori began to run to the Symphony Hall, just as Andy pulled the trigger of the Crescendo Ray. It increased the sound of Jack's lullabies at once. As Andy shot it, he felt the energy draining from his body. He quickly dropped the Crescendo Ray on the ground and rested his body against the car.

When the Crescendo Ray sounded, it did not take Desmond long to leap from the ground and knock Jack out. He was using the earplugs Dr. Maestro had made.

"Showtime's over!" he shouted at the Whisperer, dusting off his palms.

Meanwhile, Jeremy, Alice, and Marvin were running in different directions, to keep the Collectors from following Lori. She was just about to enter the Symphony Hall when Desmond saw Timbre rushing towards her. He looked around him and saw his gun by his side.

"It's been a long time since I used this," he said, quickly taking aim. When he was sure of his target, he fired. Just as Timbre was about to grab Lori, the bullet tore through his right leg, heaving him against the wall.

The sound of the gun made the Cymbals quickly turn away from the rampage they were causing at Bar Line Park. Together, they lifted into the air and saw Lori on the roof of what remained of the Symphony Hall. Furious, they headed for her.

Lori saw them coming. She raised the Baton in her hands and gave it a little tap, as if she were testing a microphone. The sound slashed the air so much that the army of Collectors cried aloud as they fell to the ground, each of them transforming back to a Pianississimo.

It was not for the Cymbals.

Their bodies crashed against the building of the Symphony Hall, tossing Lori from up above. As she fell to the ground, she swung and tapped the Baton with way more strength than she did before.

It was enough.

The Cymbals gave one last thunderous cry in the air and then fell inside the ruins of the Symphony Hall. Their cries made Lori's impact with the ground harder than it would have been. She groaned in pain and then turned her head to her left, quiet.

Andy, Desmond, Jeremy, Lola, Alice, and Marvin rushed over to where she fell and called her name.

Her silence responded.

Lola laid her head on Lori's chest and began to cry.

A car screeched near them. It was Dr. Maestro and Mark, followed by Anna McQueen, Maggie, Kelvin, and Alex Gray.

"Lori?" Dr. Maestro called, pushing Desmond and Jeremy out of his way. When he saw that Lori did not respond, he began to sob. Kelvin, watching quietly, turned and saw the Baton, lying on the ground.

He took it in his hands and held it up in the air. He was getting ready to give it a tap but stopped. He turned the device in his hand and looked at it, curious about its purpose.

"I'm alone in the world," Dr. Maestro said, lying on the ground at the side of Lori.

No one gave any attention when Kelvin softly tapped the Baton. It was a very soft tap, but it was just enough to wake Lori from the sound coma. As the sound of the Baton reached her ears, Lori's hand twitched.

Everyone was surprised.

Dr. Maestro stood up from the ground immediately.

"The Baton," he said, drawing to Kelvin who was still holding the weapon.

Desmond collected the weapon from him and tapped it softly again. Lori did not respond. Andy was the next to tap it. Still, Lori did not respond.

"It has chosen the boy," Dr. Maestro declared, collecting the Baton from Andy.

"If Lori has had contact with the Cymbals' sounds and it made her unconscious, the Baton can undo that effect. But not everyone can use it. It is the same way you were bedridden for days after using the Accelerando Whip on Larghissimo," Dr. Maestro said, looking at Mark.

"You're right about that," Andy chipped in, remembering the way he'd felt when he used the Crescendo Ray. He looked at Lori lying on the ground. He had always appreciated what she was doing for the city of Grandstaffville. But knowing now how much sacrifice she had to make each time she fought a villain, his respect for her tripled.

"Here, son," Dr. Maestro said to Kelvin, giving him the Baton. "Tap this again.

Kelvin smiled. He brought the Baton up in the air again and tapped in the air as if he were knocking on a door. The sound waves washed over Lori's body.

Everyone gasped as she coughed blood, returning to life.

Dr. Maestro placed a hand on her shoulder and wept for joy.

Lori stood up from the ground and looked around her. By now, some of the men, women, and children of Grandstaffville had gathered around. She looked at all of them, bent down, and picked up her hat, placing it on her head.

Then she spoke. "I think I'm hungry. Who's in for celebration? As I always say, 'eat and be merry and sing, for music is everywhere and in everything!'"

Everyone laughed.

Lori Biscuit, the hero of Grandstaffville, was truly back!

FINE

THE END.

www.ingramcontent.com/pod-product-compliance
Lightning Source LLC
Chambersburg PA
CBHW050408030726
47503CB00006B/2087